Jo's Search

by Paul Kropp

"Finally, my curiosity won out. There was a
chance my mother wouldn't want to see
me. There was a chance that she'd hang
up the phone on me and my life. But I had
to take that chance — otherwise my
search had been for nothing."

series
2000

PAUL KROPP

Jo's Search

Collier Macmillan Canada, Inc.

Series 2000 titles
Death Ride
Jo's Search
The Last War
The Wimp and the Jock

A **Series 2000** Teacher's Guide
is also available.

Collier Macmillan Canada, Inc.
50 Gervais Drive, Don Mills, Ontario M3C 3K4

ISBN 0-02-947370-5

GENERAL EDITOR: Paul Kropp
SERIES EDITOR: Sandra Gulland
DESIGNER: Brant Cowie
ILLUSTRATOR: Heather Collins
COVER PHOTOGRAPHY: Paterson Photographic

1 2 3 4 5 6 90 89 88 87 86
Printed and bound in Canada

CANADIAN CATALOGUING PUBLICATION DATA
Kropp, Paul, 1948-
  Jo's search

(Series 2000)
ISBN 0-02-947370-5
I. Collins, Heather. II. Title. III. Series.

PS8571.R772J6 1986   jC813'.54
C86094540-5   PZ7.K76Jo 1986

To Chris, at the other
end of these matters.

CONTENTS

CHAPTER 1

"You're just not old enough," my mom told me, as if that should be the end of it.

"I'm fifteen—two months older than Kate and she's *already* got a boyfriend."

All I wanted was a chance to go to a movie with this guy from school. It was no big deal to anybody—except my mother, of course.

"It's too soon, Jo. There's no sense rushing into things when you've got your whole life—"

"So how come Kate could go out when she was thirteen?" I broke in. I couldn't believe the way she was treating me—like I was in kindergarten.

"I'm not Kate's mother and I don't set down the rules for her," she said, wiping her hands on a towel. "I'm your mother and I don't want—"

"No, you're not," I told her, trying hard

not to cry. "You're *not* my real mother. Not at all."

Then I rushed away from the table and up the stairs, slamming my bedroom door on her and all her stupid rules. My real mother, whoever she was, wouldn't talk to me like that. She wouldn't treat me as if I was a sex-maniac for wanting to go out on a date. She'd understand what it's like to be fifteen.

But not Ruth. She was only my adoptive mother. No wonder she didn't understand me. No wonder she thought I was going to go "wild" and end up in trouble. In the back of her mind she must always have been afraid that I'd end up like my real mother. But she doesn't even know my real mother. Neither do I.

That doesn't mean I don't think about my real mom. As Ruth stomped around downstairs, I looked at myself in the mirror. But I wasn't really looking at me. I was trying to look *through* me, to see what my mother must have been like. I wondered if she had a round face like mine, or black eyes like the ones staring back at me. Or maybe I looked like my father, whoever he was. Maybe my face was like both of theirs, all mixed together. A mess.

Just like I feel.

Downstairs, I could hear the front door slam. Ruth had said she was going to the doctor—again. The car started in the driveway and I listened as it pulled away. The house was quiet. I was alone.

I walked into Jim's office to see if he had any cigarettes. Ruth won't let me smoke—so I don't tell her that I go through almost a pack a day. She'd have a fit and so would Jim.

I sat down in Jim's swivel chair and lit up. I looked around the office—the files, the computer, the big desk. Jim's an accountant for Rogers and Hyde, the biggest firm in Winnipeg. Ruth teaches grade two, so together they make piles of money—at least that's what Kate says. As if money counts for anything.

You can have all the money in the world and still feel lost if you don't know who you are. Sometimes I try to explain all that to Kate, but I don't think she understands.

She's too busy seeing her boyfriend to worry about who she is.

Who am I? I put out my cigarette and pulled out the second file drawer. My birth certificate was in there, in the "documents" file. I pulled it out and looked at the name: Josephine Martin. Martin is Jim and Ruth's last name. When you're adopted, you lose your real last name and get the one of your adoptive parents. You even get a new birth certificate to make it look like they're your real parents.

I put the birth certificate down and lit up another smoke. Something got into me, then, as I was sitting at the desk. Maybe it was just curiosity or maybe it was because I was alone in the house. Or maybe I really am a sneak, just like Ruth called me once when we were having another fight. But I decided to go through the other files to see if there was anything else in there. Anything hidden away.

I pulled out the first file drawer and got out the one marked "adoption." Jim had showed me this before—all the papers and forms that had to be filed before they could take me into their family. Ruth and Jim used to say that I was worth all the trouble, that I was "special." They don't say that much any more.

I looked through the papers but didn't see anything that I hadn't seen before. All that stuff was so official—it didn't mean anything. So I put the papers back in the folder and went to put it away. That's when I saw the envelope lying at the back of the file drawer. I picked it up and saw that it was from Truscott, the lawyer who handled my adoption.

I guess I *knew*, even then, that it was important. The envelope had no address on it—and it was sealed shut. Why? What was in there that they didn't want to see—or didn't want *me* to see?

It only took me a minute to make up my mind on what to do.

Maybe it was wrong to want to look inside. Maybe I should just have asked Jim about it to see what he said first. But I didn't want to wait—and if I told Jim, I'd just get in trouble for snooping. If there was something in the envelope about me, didn't

I have the right to know?

I went downstairs with the envelope and put the kettle on to boil. With Ruth off at the doctor's and Jim at the office, I had plenty of time.

When the kettle was steaming, I moved the envelope back and forth in front of it. In spy movies, all you have to do is put an envelope in some steam and then the flap opens right up. I stood in front of the kettle for five minutes, but the flap was still glued down. Then I put the soggy envelope down on the table and used a knife to pry up the flap.

At last I had it open. I reached inside the envelope and pulled out a single folded sheet of paper with a photograph inside. I unfolded the letter and set the photograph out on the table.

There was something strange about all this—the handwritten letter, the girl staring at me in the photograph. I felt cold, scared, as if I was doing something forbidden.

But I couldn't stop now. I couldn't not read the few words on the paper—

For my little Josephine, when you've grown up. So you'll know who I am. Hoping you'll understand, somehow.

The picture just had to be my mother—my real mother.

A girl not much older than me was standing in a backyard, looking at the camera. It was such a small picture that it was hard to make out many details—but I knew. She had my face, the same round face, the same tiny mouth that seemed to be saying ooh all the time. It looked like maybe she had my body under the coat—a little dumpy, a little too fat.

And she was looking right at me.

I bent low and studied the picture. I tried to figure out where the picture was taken, what time of year it was, how she was feeling. Was she pregnant when the picture was taken? Or had she already had me? My eyes kept coming back to her face . . . and to her smile. Who was taking her picture? Was it my father?

Then I looked at the letter, at the big, round handwriting with circles over the "i's." Three sentences. That's all she'd given me. Three sentences—eighteen words.

Was that enough?

I put the letter and picture back in the envelope and took it up to my room. I had to tell someone, and the only person who'd understand was Kate. I lay back on the bed and called her.

"You won't believe it," I said.

"Believe what?" Kate asked. I could hear her eating something noisy, like potato chips.

"Believe what I found in Jim's files."

"A partridge in a pear tree," she said. "How come you're snooping through your dad's files?"

"I wasn't snooping," I said. "I was just looking. And I found the most amazing thing."

"What?"

"A *letter* from my mother."

"From Ruth?" Kate asked.

"From my *real* mother."

Kate stopped chewing. I bet her jaw had dropped open.

"And the letter is for *me*," I explained. "It's been sitting in the file for fifteen years."

"I don't believe it," Kate said.

"There's more—a picture! A picture of her."

Of course I told Kate everything. I read her the letter four times, and described the picture to her. Kate wanted to see it and I said I'd bring it to school tomorrow. Kate understood just how I felt. She always did.

After an hour on the phone and three cigarettes in the ash tray, I heard the car come in the drive. "I better get off," I told Kate. "Ruth just drove in."

"Are you going to show her the letter?" Kate asked.

"Uhh—I think so."

"She's not going to like it. The two of you are having enough problems. Now you're going to throw this letter on top of the pile."

"But it's *my* letter," I said.

"Take my advice," Kate told me. "If you have to tell her, wait till your dad gets home. Or, better than that, don't tell them anything."

"Why should I have to make a big secret about it?" I asked her. "My birth mother

wanted me to have it."

"Then let the news wait for a little while, Jo. That's not just a letter you've got there," Kate told me.

"Then what is it?" I asked.

"It's Pandora's box."

CHAPTER 2

Pandora's box? Kate was like that, showing off things she knew that anybody else would have to look up.

I found my grade nine myth book and looked up Pandora. There she was, a girl so curious about a beautiful box that she just had to open it. Pandora opened the lid and out came all the evils of the world, like a swarm of bees.

My letter wasn't like that. My letter was a message from my mother to me. It was her way of reaching out to me, asking me to understand why she had given me up.

There was nothing bad about that, was there?

Still, I took Kate's advice and waited for Jim to get home. I needed more time to think. For all these years I had been Josie Martin, Ruth and Jim's daughter. Sure, I was adopted—but so what? I had everything I wanted all tied up in a package with a ribbon around it. But lately the ribbon had come undone. Jim and Ruth were mad at me all the time—bugging me about this, nagging me about that. Nothing seemed as simple as it used to be.

I waited until my father had come in and he had changed into his slippers. There was no sense dumping the news on him while he was still dressed in his suit for work, but I couldn't hold it in until dinner. I had to tell them.

I waited until the two of them were together in the kitchen. It was time.

"Ma, dad," I began. "I was looking in my adoption file today and I found something important."

"You've seen all that before," Ruth told me.

Jim just looked at me, his forehead all wrinkled up.

"I know," I told them. "But I wanted to look through it again and—and I found this," I said. I showed them the envelope. "It's for me."

"Jo—" Ruth began.

"That envelope is for when you're eighteen," Jim told me.

"The lawyer told us you weren't to see that until you legally became an adult," Ruth said. "It shouldn't even have been in that file."

She shot a look at Jim, as if it was all his fault.

"Well, it really was kind of under the files," I explained. "I figured it was one of the adoption papers and—"

"And you opened it," Jim said. He looked sad, but not really angry.

"You shouldn't have done that, Jo," Ruth told me.

"The letter says, 'when you've grown up,'" I told them. I knew the letter by heart —every word. "Well, I'm grown up enough."

"Mr. Truscott said you weren't to open that letter until your eighteenth birthday," Ruth told me. "In three years, the letter will be yours, Jo. Until then, I want you to give it back."

"The letter is mine," I told her, holding it tight against me. "It's *mine*."

"Jo—" she said.

It was that voice she uses that makes me feel like a five-year-old.

"There's no point, Ruth," my father broke in. "She's already opened the letter."

"There's every point," Ruth said. "And what was she doing, going through the files?" She turned to me, "Can't we trust you with anything around here?"

"But, ma—"

"I want that letter," she demanded, holding out her hand.

"I guess your mother is right," Jim said.

"She's *not*," I cried. "It's my letter and my picture and I'm not giving them back. Not ever!"

And then I ran from the kitchen.

I was crying when I got up to my room. I couldn't believe how they'd acted, what they'd said. Didn't they understand how I felt?

The first thing I did was hide the letter. I put it behind a baseboard in my closet, the same place I hide Kate's letters. They'd never find it there, not if they searched for days.

Then I threw myself on the bed. I tried not to think about how awful they made me feel. I tried to think about my birth mother. What did she tell the lawyer? What did she really want me to know?

In my heart, I knew she'd want me to have that letter now, when I needed it. I shouldn't have to wait until the calendar said I should have it. The letter wasn't a legal paper, it was a note from my mother to me. It was personal. Couldn't they understand that?

I could hear the two of them arguing down in the kitchen. I think Jim was trying to stand up for me, but it wasn't clear. Their words were muffled. It was easier to hear Ruth's screechy voice than his. And she was dead against me, I was sure of it.

Slowly their talk quieted down. At the end, I couldn't hear a thing. Then I heard Jim coming upstairs, his feet heavy as he came toward my room.

"Jo," he called, knocking on the door.

"You're not getting the letter," I shouted through the door.

"I'm not even asking for it," he said. "Can I come in?"

I flopped off my bed and opened the

door. Jim stood there in the doorway, looking very old and very tired. He had been almost forty-five when I was adopted. Now he was sixty, his hair grey, his face lined.

"Your mother and I talked about the letter, and we decided it was silly to ask for it back," he said.

"Oh?" I said. I wondered if Ruth had given in that easily.

"The letter would have been yours in three years anyway. I guess you'll just have to deal with it now."

"I wasn't snooping," I explained. "I was just going through the file."

"It doesn't matter, Jo," he told me, sitting down on the edge of the bed. "The letter is rightfully yours."

"What does Ruth say?" I asked him. I call her Ruth when I get mad at her.

"Your mother?"

"Yeah."

"Well, she's not happy about you finding the letter. But there's not much we can do about it now. Actually, we don't even know what's inside. We never knew very much about your birth mother. When you were little, you used to ask all sorts of questions that we couldn't answer."

"But you knew about the letter," I said.

"And I knew the letter was for when you were eighteen. The lawyer was very clear on that. He said that your birth mother had a lot of second thoughts about the adoption just before it went through. So he agreed to pass on an envelope to us that we could give to you. That's all I know about it. Everything else about your mother is in the adoption papers."

"But they don't say anything. My mother was Ukrainian, Catholic, and unemployed. She had no health problems. I learned more about her from one picture than from all those papers in the file."

"A picture?" Jim asked.

"There was a picture in the envelope with the letter. Of my mom."

"Your mom is downstairs, Jo, crying. For fifteen years she's loved you and cared for you. Both of us have. All this business about your birth mother only upsets Ruth," he said.

"It's got nothing to do with her," I told him.

"But it does. How do you think she feels when you two get into an argument? How do you think she feels when you remind her that she's not your birth mother?"

He looked at me with those gentle eyes of his, and I felt rotten.

"I guess—"

Jim cut me off. "I don't want to make you feel bad, Jo. I know you're curious, but try not to hurt us with it."

"It's only a letter," I said. "Don't you even want to see it?" I asked him.

"No," he told me, standing up. "If I look at it, the next thing you'll be asking me to help you find her. And I won't do that. It would be too hard on your mother. Now come on down for dinner—and let's not talk about it any more."

He smiled and went out of the room. I was left sitting at my desk, shaking my head. Not talk about it! Couldn't they see how important this was to me? Couldn't they understand that finding my mother was part of finding myself?

I went down to dinner that night and didn't say one word about the letter. But I thought about nothing else. And I knew what I had to do next. I knew I had to find my mother.

CHAPTER 3

"Was I right?" Kate asked me when I called her later that night.

"About Pandora's box?"

"No, that your mom wouldn't be happy about you reading the letter."

"She was awful," I said. "And Jim wasn't much better. He gave me all this talk about how much they loved me and how much it hurt them."

"So now you feel guilty," Kate said.

"Well, yes, I guess. But not much. I mean the letter is for me, isn't it? Maybe it's about time I found out who my mother is. I even started thinking . . . ."

"That you want to find her," Kate finished for me.

"How'd you know?"

"I've been watching it coming," Kate said. "But trying to find her won't be easy, Josie. I asked my mom about it and she said it could take a couple of years. And you might not even like what you find out. Is it worth it?"

"It doesn't matter," I told her. "I've got to do it."

I couldn't explain why. I knew it was more than just being curious. It had something to do with finding out about myself. But how could I explain that?

"In that case," Kate replied, "I'd better help you."

Kate was the perfect person to help. She was smart and tough and a better liar than anyone I knew. And if things went wrong, Kate wouldn't mind if I cried on her shoulder. She says that's what friends are for.

When I met Kate at school the next day, we traded envelopes. She couldn't wait to see the letter from my mother and the picture that came with it. I didn't know what was in the envelope she handed me.

"Parent Finders?" I asked, opening her envelope and looking inside.

"This letter is just enough to break your heart," Kate said, ignoring my question. "And your mom looks like a hippie."

"They all had long hair like that," I explained. "Now what's this?"

"Oh, it's just a booklet from this group called Parent Finders. My mom had some at work so I got one on my way to school. It'll help get us started," Kate said.

"Like where?" I asked, flipping the pages.

"Children's Aid," Kate told me. "You better read the rest of it today, because we're starting right after school."

The Child and Family Services office was in a building on Portage Avenue. I would have felt funny going there by myself, like some battered kid or runaway. But Kate was all set to come along and give me support. The booklet said that Children's Aid kept a list of adopted kids looking for their parents. They called it a registry. If my birth mother put her name on the registry too, then Children's Aid would match us up. It was all so easy.

Too easy, I found out when I got there.

"I—uh—I'd like to find my mother," I told the lady at the desk.

She just gave me a funny look. I realized that what I said must have sounded strange.

"My friend is an adopted child," Kate explained, "and she'd like to register to find her birth mother." The way she talks, I think Kate is going to be a lawyer.

"Oh, of course," said the woman at the desk. "I'll call Ms. Adams."

I smiled. I felt as if we might really be getting somewhere. We were sent to an office down the hall. Inside was a tall woman with streaks of grey in her hair. She asked if she could help us and this time I spoke for myself.

"I'm adopted, but I'd like to find my birth mother," I said.

"You understand that putting your name in the registry doesn't always work," Ms. Adams said. "Only about four out of ten people do find their birth parents."

"Lousy odds," I mumbled.

"I'm afraid so. Not all birth parents want to make contact with their children. They have a right to privacy if they want it. That's why we have the registry. Both sides have to want to meet each other."

"What if my mother doesn't know about this match-up thing?"

"Then the registry won't work," she said. "We can match you up with anyone who's listed in Manitoba. But if your mother hasn't put her name in here, well . . . ."

"It's worth a try," Kate said when she saw my spirits sag.

"I guess," I told them both. "How long will it take?"

"About six months," Ms. Adams said, reaching in her desk for some papers.

"Six months!" I cried.

"And that's the earliest," she went on. "Sometimes it takes a year. We have quite a backlog."

Kate and I just looked at each other. There was nothing we could do to make the system work any faster.

"Now if you'll just take these forms home and fill out the information," Ms. Adams said. "Get your adoptive parents to sign here." She put two X's on the form.

"Uh . . . do they have to?" I asked.

"Unless you're eighteen, we'll need their permission to go ahead. You've told them about your search?" she asked.

"Oh, of course," I said, but I think she

knew I was lying even then.

"Well, then there won't be any problem," Ms. Adams said, smiling at me.

I felt like choking. There was no way I could get Ruth and Jim to sign those papers. I couldn't even tell them about wanting to find my mother. They'd be "hurt." They'd be angry. And they'd do whatever they could to stop me.

"It won't work," I told Kate when we got out of the office.

"I could maybe sign the forms for you," she said.

"And get yourself in real trouble? Besides, they might call the house to check. Then we'd both be found out. My goose would be cooked for looking for my mom. And yours would be roasted for forging their names."

"I guess it's not worth it," Kate sighed. "And even if it worked, you've still got less than a fifty-fifty chance."

"And it would take six months," I said.

"To a year," Kate added.

Then we fell silent. The whole thing looked rotten. My search had begun and ended in two days. And I was nowhere. I began to think it would have been better if I'd never found the envelope. But it was too late now. I couldn't close up my mother's letter and forget about her. I just had to find out more—and I wanted to find out fast.

It was Kate who came up with an answer. We were on the bus, and I was just staring out the window at the snow coming down. Christmas was a month away. I'd be getting all sorts of stuff from Ruth and Jim, anything that money could buy. But not what I really wanted. What I really wanted was to find my mother.

"I've got an idea," Kate said. She was reading through the Parent Finders' booklet.

"Yeah?"

"There is somebody who might know where to find your mother—the lawyer who handled your adoption. Where's that envelope?" she demanded.

"Here it is," I said, reaching into my purse.

Kate looked at the return address. "Sterling, Monihan, and Truscott," she said.

"It's Truscott," I said. "His name is all over the adoption papers."

"That's the man to talk to. I bet he knows everything you need to know."

I knew Kate was right—that Truscott had some answers. But I wondered if he'd give them to me. He was Ruth and Jim's lawyer, not mine. And neither of them were on my side.

Ruth was waiting for me when I got home. She seemed more upset than angry when I came in.

"You're a bit late," she sighed.

"I went downtown," I told her. "With Kate." That much was true—I didn't want to lie.

"Christmas shopping?" she asked.

"Uh, sort of," I said. Now I was lying. What I wanted to say was, *I was searching for my birth mother*. That would have been honest and open and fair. But I couldn't tell her that.

"I'm sorry about yesterday," she said, forcing a smile. "Sometimes I get upset and say things I shouldn't."

I looked up and felt sorry for her. She looked tired and upset. I could feel the hurt. Now if only I could feel love . . . .

"It's O.K.," I said. I almost called her mom, but something stopped me.

I stood there, feeling awkward. I think both of us wanted to say more, but it was too hard.

I turned away and went up to my room. I felt a whole bunch of emotions walking upstairs—regret, guilt, sadness. Maybe those feelings were the ones Pandora had let out of the box.

CHAPTER

The next afternoon, Kate and I went down to Truscott's office. It was in an old house that had been turned into lawyers' offices. On the outside was a brass sign: "Sterling, Monihan, and Truscott, Barristers and Solicitors."

"What's a barrister?" I asked Kate.

"A lawyer," she said.

"Then why don't they call themselves lawyers?"

"If you charge two hundred dollars an hour for your time, you can call yourself anything you want," Kate replied. "My mom says that Truscott is the oldest lawyer in Winnipeg."

"Did she say anything else?" I asked.

"Nothing that wouldn't get you upset," Kate told me.

We walked into the front hall and stared around at the office. The walls were panelled in wood, and the ceiling had designs in the plaster. A receptionist sat at a desk in front of us.

"I'd like to see Mr. Truscott, please," I told the receptionist.

"Do you have an appointment?" she asked.

"No, but it won't take very long."

"I'm afraid Mr. Truscott is booked with clients this afternoon."

"Well, it's important," I said. The woman was giving me a look like I was from some other planet.

"Could I ask what the nature of your business is?" she asked coldly.

"It's about my adoption," I said, trying to find the right words. "Mr. Truscott handled the legal papers and . . . uh, I'd like to talk to him. Just for a minute or two."

"Well, I can't promise that he'll see you," she said.

"Could you just ask him? My name is Josephine Martin. Tell him I only need a minute of his time."

"Just have a seat, please."

Kate and I went over to a big leather

42

couch. She whispered something to me about making an appointment to see Truscott. But that would just put everything off. I wanted to see him now. If he wasn't going to tell me anything, I wanted to know right away.

After a couple of minutes, Kate nudged me. She pointed to a picture on the wall of a man who looked a hundred years old. I looked at the caption: "Jerome C. Truscott." So that was Truscott—maybe the only person who knew where I could find my mother.

I sat there another fifteen minutes before I heard my name: "Miss Martin, please." I jumped off the couch and went up to the receptionist's desk.

"Miss Martin, I'm afraid Mr. Truscott can't see you today," she said. "His schedule is quite full. He also asked me to tell you that the firm's policy on adoption cases is quite clear. He can't give you any information that is not in the public record. Now, if you'd like to see him on any other matter, I can make an appointment," she added.

"But I just wanted to ask him a question," I said.

"If it's about your adoption, I'm afraid he can't discuss the matter. The court records are sealed, Miss Martin."

"I know that, but—"

"Now if there's any other way he can help you . . . ."

"No . . . I guess not. Oh, never mind," I said.

I couldn't even look at Kate. I just hid my eyes and rushed out of the office.

Kate was beside me on the street. I knew she was worried about me. She had said that I was pinning too much hope on the search. She had told me that I might get hurt. And of course she was right.

"My mom said that would happen," Kate told me.

"But Truscott knows," I cried.

"What good is knowing if he won't talk. I mean, he won't even see you, Jo. We're stumped."

"Not yet," I told her. "I'll . . . ." My voice died out.

"You'll what?"

"I'm not going to give up just because Truscott doesn't want to see me. I'll make him see me. I'll—"

"That's it," Kate said. "We can wait him out. We'll sit in the coffee shop over there until he comes out."

"And then I'll pounce on him," I said, feeling hopeful again.

The waiting was the worst part. We sat in the coffee shop until five, talking about Truscott and lawyers and whether Kate should dump her boyfriend. I was chain smoking to pass the time. But still there was no sign of him.

By 5:30, I began wondering if there was some other door out of the lawyers' offices. By 6:00, I was out of smokes and Kate was ready to give up and go home.

But I wasn't.

The longer I waited, the angrier I got. I felt like Truscott and my parents and Children's Aid were all against me. But I was going to beat them. I was going to beat all of them and find my mom.

It was almost 6:30 when Truscott finally came out. I jumped up and ran across from the coffee shop, ready to chase him if I had to. But Truscott was an old man who walked with a cane. There was no way he could get away from me.

"Mr. Truscott," I said.

"Yes?" he answered, turning toward me.

"I'm Josephine Martin. I tried to see you this afternoon."

"Yes—I remember," he said. "I asked the receptionist to explain the problem to you."

By this time, Kate had paid our bill and caught up to me. I was really glad she was there.

"All I got was the firm's policy, Mr. Truscott."

"I'm sorry, but I can't do any better than that."

"Look," I said, reaching into my purse and pulling out the envelope. "My mother wanted me to have this. It tells me something about her, but not enough. I've *got* to find her, Mr. Truscott. You've got to give me something more to go on. Just her name. Or anything."

The old man shook his head. "This kind of case breaks my heart, but there's nothing I can do."

"But you *must* have her name in your files," I cried.

"No doubt we do," Truscott said. "But an adoption is sealed by law. And I'm an officer of the court. If I told you any more, it would mean breaking my word to serve the will of the court."

"But . . . . "

"Mr. Truscott," Kate came in when I ran out of words, "surely you can think of something to help."

"I'm afraid my hands are tied," Truscott said. "If you can't wait for the registry, then use the information you have to find out what you need. Maybe that letter has more in it than you realize."

"But—"

"I've already said more than I should," Truscott told us. "Good evening, and good luck to you, Josephine."

I just stood there with Kate, stunned, watching Truscott turn and walk slowly back to the parking lot.

"We're nowhere," I moaned.

He had said nothing at all, nothing that would help.

.

CHAPTER **5**

"I got us some help," Kate told me over the phone.

It was a week after our visit to Truscott, three weeks before Christmas. I didn't have any Christmas spirit. Ruth and Jim were sure I was sneaking around seeing guys. But it wasn't guys I had on my mind—it was finding my real mom. And how could I tell them that?

"What help?" I asked her.

"Help to find your birth mother, you jerk," Kate told me. "I talked my mom into helping you."

"You think I need a social worker?" I said. Maybe I was a little upset these days, but I didn't think it was that bad.

"No, we need her brains. Bring over everything you have on your adoption. Maybe she'll have an idea."

I figured my search was worth one more

try. When I got to Kate's house, I spread the envelope, the letter, the picture, and my adoption papers on the kitchen table. Then we got started.

"So this is everything you know?" Kate's mother asked.

"Yeah. My whole life doesn't even take up half a kitchen table," I said with a laugh.

Kate just shook her head. "The question is what do we need to know to find your mother. Where do we start?"

"With a name?" I asked.

"That's right," Kate's mom told us. "You need her name before you can even start to locate where she is now. If only she'd signed the letter."

"All we know is that she's Ukrainian, Catholic, and that maybe she lived here in Winnipeg."

"Wait a minute," Kate's mother said. "I think 'Catholic' might be something to go on. Since you were born a Catholic, Josie, there's a good chance that you were baptized."

"So?" I said.

"I see it," Kate jumped in. "If you were

baptized, some church in town will have a record of it."

"And that record will have your mother's name," her mom said.

"But where do we go first? There must be thirty Catholic churches in town," I said.

We all fell silent, thinking. I knew we were on to something, but what?

"The picture," I cried out. "There's a smokestack in the picture. If we can figure out where that is, then maybe all I have to do is check the churches in that area."

"Great," Kate agreed. "I'll get a magnifying glass."

Kate ran up to her room while her mother and I looked at the photograph. There wasn't much to go on—some trees, a house or two. Mostly the picture showed my mother in a backyard.

"I've got it," Kate said, coming back with the magnifying glass. She bent over the picture and stared hard through the lens. "Somebody write this down. W . . . A . . . blur . . . S . . . T . . . A . . . and then there's a tree."

I started playing with the letters, trying to

make a word. "Wanstall? Wabstar?"

"Wagstaff," Kate's mother told us. "It used to be a factory in the east end. I remember when it was torn down a few years ago. It's just the other side of St. John's Park."

"Let's check the phone book. There can't be that many churches over there," Kate said.

She was right. In fifteen minutes, we knew that there were only three churches even close to where the factory used to be. That made my work simple—*if* my birth mother had gone ahead and had me baptized at one of them.

"When do we check them out?" Kate asked.

"Tomorrow," I said, "after school."

The next day, Kate and I rode the bus over to St. John's Park. We could see the big Catholic church only a block away, just down a street of little shops. I was too busy thinking about the church and what I would say there to pay attention to the stores. It was Kate who stopped me.

"Hey, look in there," she said.

"Look at what?"

"Those china hearts, Josie. See, they've got that Ukrainian design on the outside. That'd be a nice present for your mother, don't you think?"

"Which mother?" I sighed. "Come on, let's get to the church."

A big Catholic church was only a block away. I didn't know quite what to do when we actually got to St. Ann's. I ran up the steps to the big doors at the front, but they were locked. We tried them all.

Then we went around to the back to see if there was another entrance. Instead, we found a brick building attached to the church. I pushed the doorbell and we waited.

Finally a voice came from inside.

"I'm coming . . . I'm coming."

There were several clicks as locks came off the inside of the door. Then the door swung open. In front of me was a very old priest, dressed in a long black robe.

"Yes, ladies?" he asked, squinting at the two of us.

"I, uh, I'd like to ask about my baptism certificate," I said.

"Baptism will be next Sunday," he said. "Just bring your son or daughter . . . ." Then he stopped. I think he finally figured out how old we were.

"No, Father. You see, Josie needs a new baptism *certificate*," Kate said. She raised her voice since he seemed to be a little deaf.

"Oh, a certificate . . . yes, yes. Were you baptized here at St. Ann's?"

"I think so."

"Then come in, come in. Let me just open the files and we'll have this all straightened out in no time. No time at all. A baptism certificate . . . and I thought you . . . Oh."

He wasn't really talking to me or to Kate, so we didn't say anything back. He led us into a small, yellow-painted office.

"Just have a seat, for a moment. I'll go over to the files here," he said, walking very slowly. "Now what is your name, please."

"Josephine."

"And I am Father Anselm," he said, smiling. "It is so nice having you young people visiting."

"Thank you, Father Anselm," I said,

trying to get him back on track. "I'm not sure just when I was baptized, but I can give you my date of birth."

"Well, well. We may just have to look through the book, then. Now what is your birth date?"

I told him when I was born. He opened up a large book and ran his fingers down the pages. "And what was your name again?" he asked.

"My first name is *Josephine*, Father," I told him.

"Let me try again," he said. "Josephine . . . hmmm, in September . . . here's a Josephine," he said, stopping his finger at an entry in the book. "The birthday is right, but . . . oh, these old eyes of mine. Let me get my glasses here from the drawer."

He pulled out a pair of wire-rim glasses and put them on. "Now I can see clearly, yes, indeed."

Kate and I exchanged a look. The old priest made both of us smile.

"Yes. Here you are . . . Josephine . . . now . . . oh, yes, of course. Josephine Markovic, right there in front of my eyes.

That is your name, isn't it?"

Markovic. That was my name! That had been my name the day I was born. That had been the name of my real mother. And now it was mine again.

"Let's just check the birthdate to be sure," he said. "September 13?"

"That's right," I told him.

"Yes, yes," the old priest said. "And your mother was Katrina. I think I remember your family . . . or was it . . . ? Oh, all that was so long ago."

Kate stood up and went over to Father Anselm. I couldn't stand up—my mind was spinning. *Katrina Markovic!* I had her name —my mother's name.

"Well, well," Father Anselm went on. "And you need a new certificate."

"Uh, yes," I said. That was my story so I had to follow through on it. What I really wanted was to go running out of the church, shouting my mother's name.

But I held myself in. I waited while old Father Anselm found a fountain pen, slowly found a baptism certificate and carefully filled it in. It felt like he took an hour for all that, but I didn't care. At last I held the paper in my hand. Father Anselm walked Kate and me to the door.

"Now, Josephine, you take better care of this one than you did of the first," the old priest said.

"Uh, yes, Father," I said.

"Give it to your mother, for safe-keeping," he said, smiling at me.

"Yes, I will, Father," I said.

But that wouldn't be as easy as either of us thought.

CHAPTER 6

Josephine Markovic. That was all I could think about—my name, my mother, me. As Kate and I walked up the street, I was bubbling over inside. I had found the signature to my mother's letter! Almost as if I knew the girl in the picture. Things were finally beginning to fall together.

"Josie," Kate said, breaking into my thoughts. "While you were getting all gaga over your mother, I was reading the register over Father Anselm's shoulder."

"Yeah?" I said.

"There's another column in the register where they put the father's name."

"So?"

"Yours was blank," Kate said. "You know what that means, don't you?"

"I'm not sure."

"Well, I don't know if we should really talk about this right now. But I'd guess that your mom got pregnant and the guy didn't want to marry her. It's just like a soap opera."

I felt embarrassed, as if I had anything to do with it. "Maybe *she* didn't want to marry *him*," I said.

"There's only one way to find out," Kate said. "You've got to track down Katrina Markovic. Then you can ask her yourself."

"Really?" I said. We seemed so close to finding my mother that suddenly I felt scared at the idea.

"Sure. Meet me at the library tomorrow morning. We'll use that Parent Finders booklet and have her tracked down in no time."

I told Ruth and Jim I was going down to the library to work on a project. It felt good to be able to tell them the truth, even if it wasn't the whole truth.

Ruth even drove me downtown since she was going Christmas shopping. Riding with her in the car, she told me about some medical problems she had. She was going to have a small operation after Christmas, and she was upset about it. She'd been keeping the whole thing a secret from Jim and me.

I felt bad for her. I guess we had both been keeping secrets, but I wasn't ready to share mine yet. Ruth had enough problems without that.

I got out of the car at the library and met Kate up in the reference room. Kate said that we needed the old city directories. We started with the directory from seventeen years ago. My mother wouldn't even have known then that she would get pregnant and have me. She was probably just a teenager, like me.

The back of the directory listed all the family names in Winnipeg. There were seven Markovics, but none of them was Katrina or Katherine or even just K. Markovic.

"So what now?" I wondered.

"She probably lived with your grandparents. Let's check each of the addresses. That should narrow it down."

Kate went over and got a city map from the librarian. We checked each of the seven addresses. Five of them were in the wrong part of town. Maybe they were relatives of mine, but none of the listings had a child who could be my mother. Then we checked the two Markovics who lived near St. Ann's church. One Markovic, an accountant, lived alone. Not much chance there. The other, Walter Markovic, lived on Rosemount Street, about two blocks from St. Ann's. He had a wife and two children—and one child was listed as Katrina.

"Walter's your grandfather," Kate said, grinning.

"And there's my mother. How funny. I've learned more about myself in the last two days than I have in the last fifteen years."

"Now we'll just check the directories for each year up to now. If your family has stayed put, the rest is easy."

But it wasn't. Three years later, Walter Markovic was living only with his wife. Katrina, my mother, and Tom, my uncle, must have grown up and left home. What's worse, neither of them stayed in Winnipeg. There were no new Markovics in any of the listings.

Then we lost all of them. When we looked in the directory from five years ago,

there were no Markovics on Rosemount at all. We had hit a dead end.

"What happened?" I asked, really just thinking out loud.

"Maybe your grandparents died?" Kate suggested.

That gave me a funny feeling inside. *Maybe I'll never know them*, I thought. For a half-hour, while we pored over the directories, my family had come alive. Now they had disappeared. Maybe they were dead—my mother too. And the whole search would bring me nothing more than names on paper.

"Let's work some more on your mother," Kate said. I think she understood how I felt. "It looks like she either moved or got married thirteen years ago."

"If she got married, it might be in the paper," I said, feeling hopeful again. "Then we can search using her new name."

Now we had to use the microfilm machines. Kate took the microfilms for the first part of that year. I took the second part. Day by day, we cranked the film to the "Marriage" listing. All this was boring and took us three hours.

And we came up with nothing.

"Are you sure you checked every paper?" I asked her. "If you missed even one day—"

"You want to do my half over again?" Kate asked. I think she was as tired and cranky as I was.

"Well, what now?"

"Maybe she didn't get married. Maybe your mother just moved to another city," Kate said. "We could check some other city directories."

Kate was trying to be hopeful, but I had an awful, sinking feeling in my heart. I looked around at the rows of city directories, at the stacks of microfilm, and I shook my head. Maybe if we searched everything, we'd find the clue we needed. But it would take forever. There had to be some faster way.

"I've got an idea," Kate said.

"Yeah?"

"Let's have something to eat, then we'll take the bus to Rosemount Street and snoop around."

"That's how all this got started," I told

her. "My snooping got me Pandora's box. Lifting the lid let out all the troubles we've been having," I sighed. And that's how I felt. Maybe I would have been better off if I had never seen my mother's letter.

"Yeah, but there's another part of the Pandora myth that you forgot," Kate said.

"What's that?"

"The box had all the evils of the world, but it had one good thing, too." She waited a second before telling me what the good thing was. "It was hope, Josie. Pandora gave us hope."

CHAPTER 7

I didn't have all that much hope when Kate and I got off the bus near St. Ann's. We walked up Main Street, past the old butcher shops and dress stores with signs in three languages. Then we reached Rosemount.

Kate and I walked down to number 37, my grandparents' house. There wasn't much to the place. It was a small bungalow with grey stucco on the outside. The front yard was small, but the backyard stretched quite a ways. Looking down the laneway, I wondered if that was where the picture had been taken. There was a gate that led to the back, but no lock on it. The house itself seemed pretty empty.

"You want to go in back?" Kate asked, reading my mind.

"Yeah," I told her. "I've got the picture here in my purse."

Kate went first and unlatched the gate.

Then the two of us walked to the back of the house. I took out my mom's picture and compared it to the backyard. There was no smokestack, the bushes were bigger and now there was snow on the ground. But everything else seemed to fit—the houses in back, the stone path under my feet. Even the pine tree was in the right place, though it was much bigger now than it was in the photo.

"This is the right place," Kate said, looking over my shoulder.

I tried to put myself where the photographer stood when the snapshot was taken. When I was in the right spot, I pictured my mom where she stood in the photograph. It was almost as if she was there, right in front of me, smiling the way she did in the picture. And if only she could, my mom would come to life and talk to me.

"Something I can do for you?"

I snapped out of my dream as soon as I heard the voice. Behind us, at the gate, stood an older man with greying hair.

"I . . . uh, oh, I'm sorry," I said.

"We were just passing by," Kate said. "My friend's family lived here and she wanted to look at the old yard." Kate didn't sound as scared and surprised as I was.

"I just wondered," the old man said.

"Do you live here?" Kate asked.

"No, next door. The Koski's are away so I'm looking after the house. You two relatives of theirs?"

"Well, no, not really. You see, this used to be my grandparents' house," I explained.

"So you're one of the Markovics, eh?" the old man said, smiling for the first time.

"Maybe you knew her mother," Kate said. "Katrina Markovic?"

"I knew the whole family. Been living here at number 39 for thirty years now. So you've come back to visit the old house, eh? Your mom still in Calgary?"

"Yes, she is," Kate answered for me. I'm always amazed at the way she can lie with such a straight face.

"Haven't seen your mom or your uncle Tom for a million years. Kind of sad how you lose touch with people."

"That's true," I said. Very true.

"Of course, everybody moves around these days. When your mom married Stephen Novak, the first thing they did was move out of town."

"Novak?" Kate asked. But then she realized that we should know the name. The old guy didn't seem to hear her anyway. "Oh, right, uh Mrs. Novak said she loved growing up here."

"You see much of your uncle Tom?" he asked.

"Oh, not too much," I said.

"Well, you tell him and your mom that Mr. Kostash next door said hello."

"Sure thing."

"And wish her a Merry Christmas."

"I will," I told him. *And just maybe I would*, I thought. There was so much I wanted to ask him, but I was afraid I would give us away.

He turned and went back to his house while Kate and I walked to the street. Kate was grinning. "You've found her!" she cried.

"Well, almost," I said.

"What more do you need? Stephen Novak in Calgary. One call to information should give you the number. And then, well, you could see her at Christmas."

"All this is happening so fast," I told her.

"What's wrong, Jo?" Kate asked. "Don't you want to meet your mother?"

"Well, yes, but . . . maybe it's not all that simple."

And it wasn't—I knew that even then. In the days that followed, I kept thinking about how complicated it was. Ruth and Jim didn't even know I was looking for my mom. How would they take it if I said I wanted to see her? They'd go right through the roof. They might even forbid me to see her. What would I do then?

And what if my mother didn't want to see me? I tried to think of things from her point of view. She had a new life with a husband who might not even know about me. Maybe I would be an embarrassment to her. Maybe I was part of her life that she was trying to forget. What's more, I had no way of checking to see if my mother had been looking for me. Maybe it would be better just to wait until I was eighteen and use the registry.

But another part of me didn't want to wait. I had searched hard for her. I had wanted to meet her—because I wanted to get in touch with her and with myself. Didn't I have a right to my own past? Didn't I have a right to know why she put me up for adoption, or who my father was?

My curiosity won out. I couldn't know how my mother felt about me unless I called her. I had to take the chance—even if she hung up on me and wanted to keep me out of her life. I had to risk it, to bury my fears and call her.

I waited for a night when Ruth and Jim were going out shopping. When they left, I went up to my room and got ready. I had called information before and I had the number in my desk. I took a deep breath and dialed.

The phone in Calgary rang and a boy answered. "May I speak to Mrs. Novak, please," I said.

"Just a minute," the boy grunted. I could hear him shouting "Mom" out into the house. I realized that he must be my stepbrother.

Stay calm, I told myself.

"Hello," I heard on the other end of the line. It was a woman's voice. My mother's voice.

"Hello," I said back, trying to keep my voice steady. "Is this Katrina Novak who used to live on Rosemount Street in Winnipeg?"

"Yes. Is something wrong?" she asked.

"Well, no," I said, searching for words. "I . . . uh . . . don't really know how to say this. Did you have a baby girl in September, fifteen years ago?" I broke off. I was losing control.

"Oh, my goodness . . . . Is that you, Josephine?" she asked. Her voice was breaking up.

"Yes, it's me," I said. *Your daughter*, I wanted to add.

"Oh, this is wonderful," she said. It sounded like she was crying now. "Wonderful."

And then I began crying with her. The two of us were half-crazy, crying and laughing at the same time. I guess I had been building up so much inside me. All this time, wanting to talk to her and being so afraid that she wouldn't want to talk to me.

We talked and talked, for almost an hour. There was so much we both wanted to know. She thought I had gotten her number from the adoption registry. I had to explain how I had found her, and what my life was like, and all about Ruth and Jim. There was so much to say—fifteen years to catch up on.

And there was so much for me to find out. I had a real mother, one who worked as a legal secretary in Calgary. I had a step-father and two step-brothers who lived in the suburbs with two dogs, a cat, and a goldfish named Cleo. I had two grandparents who had died in a car crash five years ago. I had an uncle, cousins, everything.

I kept grabbing at the bits and pieces of my life and my family. It was like pieces in a jigsaw puzzle, but the puzzle was my life. Each piece made it more whole, more real.

"And what about my father?" I asked her.

"Oh, I don't want to talk about that on

the phone," my mother said. "I'll tell you about it when you get here. Can you visit us over the Christmas holidays? It would be such a wonderful time for all of us."

"Well, I don't know," I said, thinking suddenly of Ruth and Jim. "I can ask."

"Don't worry about a thing. We'll take care of the plane ticket and you can stay right here. Just ask your parents and call me back."

"Oh, sure," I said. *Ask my parents*. I guess that meant Ruth and Jim. I hadn't been thinking about them as my parents that much. I'd been so confused about them and me and what we meant to each other. Yet Ruth and Jim still were my parents, legally, and maybe in other ways too. How would they feel when I told them about my mom?

CHAPTER 8

"You finally called her?" Kate asked. I phoned her right after talking to my mother.

"I did!" I cried. "And she wants me to come visit. She sounds so *nice*, Kate, I can hardly believe it."

"So it was easier than you thought?" Kate wanted to know.

"She's been looking for me through the registry. She's been hoping for years that I'd get in touch with her. And now she wants me to come to Calgary during the Christmas break."

"That's pretty fast. What will your parents say?"

"I, uh, I haven't told them yet," I admitted.

"Well, don't get your hopes up, Josie. This isn't going to be easy," Kate said.

Nor would it get any easier if I waited to tell them. I talked to Kate about it and she thought I might as well tell the truth.

I had found my birth mother—and now I wanted to see her. It was as simple as that. It didn't mean that I no longer loved Ruth and Jim.

But would they know that?

I heard the two of them come in downstairs. I was nervous about going down to tell them.

And I was worried. They'd been good parents. Kate always said that they spoiled me. She said that I got more love and attention as an adopted kid than I would if I had been theirs naturally.

In so many ways I was their real daughter. Never once, not even in all the fights we had, did they remind me that I was adopted. I was *their* daughter, not some kid they picked up off the shelf. And I guess I loved them for that, and for everything else, though sometimes it was hard to tell them.

Now I had to break the hardest news to them. Jim had said he wouldn't help me look for my mom, but that didn't mean I couldn't do it myself. He had said he didn't want to talk about it, but we couldn't keep silent any more.

I found Ruth reading a magazine down in the living room.

"Ma—" I began. "I've got to talk to you and dad about something. Something important."

"What's all this?" Jim asked, coming out of the kitchen. He had a glass of egg nog in his hand.

"I've got to talk to you about, well, it's about my birth mother."

The two of them looked at each other. The smiles disappeared from their faces. The lines on Jim's forehead grew deeper. He looked worried.

I know I was.

"I don't really know how to say this," I began.

"It has to do with that letter, doesn't it?" Jim asked. He put his arm around Ruth, as if he knew what I was going to say.

"Yes, but it goes back before then," I tried to explain. "You remember I used to ask questions about her even when I was a little girl. I guess the questions just don't go away. But the letter, well, it gave me some information I needed," I said, biting my lip. "You see, I've found her. She's in Calgary, and I talked to her tonight."

"Oh, my," was all Ruth could say.

"We knew it would happen sooner or later," Jim told her.

"I know, but . . . so soon."

The two of them looked so upset that I felt awful. I had to say something, something to make them understand.

"It's not as bad as you think," I began. "Her name is Katrina Novak now. She's got her own family. She lives in Calgary and she's a secretary and she's got two children of her own. And me, well, I've got my own family too. That's you."

I looked at the two of them and tried to think of something else to say. I just didn't want them to feel hurt.

Jim spoke up before I could say anything more.

"Josie," he said, "your mom and I have been doing a lot of talking since the day you found the letter. I think I said some things to you that night that . . . ."

He bit his lower lip. I'd never seen my dad have to fight back tears before.

"Well, I was wrong," he said. "We decided that you had every right to find your birth mother. It wasn't an easy decision, let me tell you."

"But we finally understood what it meant to you," Ruth said, picking up where my dad left off. "So we . . . ." And then she couldn't speak.

Jim went ahead. "We went to Truscott and . . . well, I guess we have one Christmas gift you don't need anymore," he said.

He reached under the tree and passed me a small package. I just held it in my hand, not sure what I was supposed to do with it.

"Open it, Josie," he said.

I pulled off the ribbon and ripped away the paper. Then I opened the box inside and saw a set of legal forms—the same ones I'd seen at Children's Aid. These were the papers to get me on the match-up registry— all filled out and signed.

"You see," Jim went on, his voice cracking, "we didn't want to stand in your way."

And then all of us—*all of us*—started to cry.

"I'm always going to love you two," I told them, tears falling down my cheeks.

Jim came over and put his arm around me. "We know that, Josie. Of course we know that. It's just hard, that's all, all this happening so soon."

"I don't want to hurt you. I mean, you're my family, my *real* family."

"Do you really feel that?" Ruth asked me.

"More than ever," I told her. And I wasn't lying to them.

Maybe the one thing that talking to my birth mother had done was to make her real to me. She wasn't a dream any more. She wasn't some perfect mother living in never-never-land. She was a woman with two kids and a husband living in Calgary. She was important, and she was a part of me, but not like Jim and Ruth.

My real mother was standing next to me, crying. She needed me, then, just as I have needed her for all the years before.

So I put my arms around her.

"It's all right, ma. I want to go visit her

after Christmas, but I'll be back. I'll be right here with you."

"Promise?" she asked.

"Promise," I told them both.

CHAPTER 9

I was in a buzz for the week before I went out to Calgary. I kept imagining what it would be like to see my mother. Would it be as easy as it had been on the phone? Would we be awkward or embarrassed? Kate said it would be a mix of all the feelings I had.

Jim and Ruth kept reminding me that, whatever happened, they'd be waiting for me. And they said it was O.K. for me to start dating in the new year. I was glad to hear both those things, though right now, boys were the last thing on my mind.

Jim and Ruth came with me to the airport. The three of us hugged before I got on the plane. Ruth was trying to be strong, but I could see her crying as I started down the ramp. I knew that part of her felt I would never come back, that she was losing her daughter.

I sat on the plane to Calgary thinking

about my birth mother—and worrying about Jim and Ruth.

Why was it all so complicated?

At last the plane landed in Calgary. As I carried my overnight bag up the ramp I could see a small crowd of people waiting at the top. But I couldn't see anyone who looked like my mother.

I walked into the airport lobby and stood, waiting. All around me, people were meeting, hugging each other. Others were smiling and shouting "Merry Christmas." I just waited, worrying that maybe she changed her mind. It felt like forever.

When almost everyone had gone, a woman came walking up to me. She was wearing a heavy winter coat and hat.

"Josephine?" the woman asked, smiling.

I looked at her and I knew. "Mom," I cried.

She held me in her arms for the first time in fifteen years.

We were both crying ... because, well, because of everything.

She was so much older, now, than her picture. There were lines around her eyes

and she had put on a little weight. But her smile was the same, and it welcomed me back to her.

That weekend I got to know my mother. In her letter, she had wanted me to understand, somehow, why she had given me up. By the end of the weekend, it made sense. She had been seventeen when she got pregnant. My father was a boy named Frankie Marriot, the drummer in a rock band. They were in love, my mother said, but she knew it was impossible for them to raise a family. Frankie was still a kid, still dreaming of becoming another Ringo Starr. When she got pregnant, her parents wanted to kick her out. My father went off on tour and never came back from Toronto. My mom was alone and desperate. So my grandfather used the family lawyer to arrange an adoption.

Fifteen years had taken us all a long way from each other, but Katrina Novak was still my mother in so many ways. Not only did we look much the same, but we had the same problems with fat hips and trying to diet. We both gave in to tears too easily, both laughed too loud, both took tea with no cream or sugar.

There were so many little things that connected us together that it was hard to believe I had just met her.

But that, too, was the truth. Katrina Novak was my mother, my birth mother, but we each had our own families. I saw her with her two boys, Tim and John, and understood that this was her real family. Just as my real family was back in Winnipeg.

The plane brought me back to Winnipeg on the day before school started.

Ruth and Jim were waiting for me in the airport lobby. They looked nervous, as if they feared I had changed. And maybe I had. Maybe I had finally come to terms with needing my mother, but loving the two of them.

I ran over to where they stood and threw my arms around Ruth first.

"I'm back, just like I promised," I said to them both.

My mother relaxed in my arms and I knew she felt glad that I was there.

"Did the visit go all right?" Jim asked with a nervous smile.

"Just fine," I said. "I'll have to visit her again."

Jim looked at me, a flash of panic in his eyes.

"In the summer sometime," I told him. "She's busy working and looking after her kids, so I think we'll be writing more than visiting. But look, I have something for you. It's in my suitcase. Sort of a late Christmas present."

I opened up my suitcase and pulled out a wrapped box. I had bought it before I left—for my birth mother—but somehow it didn't feel right for her.

"It's really for you," I said, handing it to Ruth.

"I feel silly," she said, holding the box like it was going to break.

"Oh, go ahead and open it," I said, grinning at her. "I think you'll be glad to get it."

So she pulled off the wrapping and

opened the box. Beneath the wrapping paper was the china heart with a Ukrainian design on the top. It was the heart that Kate had pointed out in the store near St. Ann's.

I had bought the heart to give to my mother—my real mother.

And that's why I had to bring it back home.

About the Author

Paul Kropp lives in Hamilton, Ontario, where he began writing *Series Canada* in 1978. He has three sons — two now in high school and a third just out of kindergarten. In addition to fifteen of the books in *Series Canada,* he has written *Getting Even,* a young-adult novel published by Bantam/Seal. His interests include piano, tennis, bicycling, photography, politics, and — of all things — croquet.

Acknowledgements

The author would like to thank Chris Bouchel and Michael Nash.

Other titles in Series 2000

DEATH RIDE
by Paul Kropp

Tim wanted to get in on the action — the drugs, the booze, and all that went with it. He wanted to break out from his boring life and take it right to the edge. He didn't know that one more joyride would lead to death.
ISBN 02-947360-8

THE LAST WAR
by Martyn Godfrey

Brad was one of the lucky ones. He survived the bomb, and he believes that someday all will be the same again. But then he meets Angel, who shows him what it really means to be a survivor of the last war.
ISBN 02-947380-2

THE WIMP AND THE JOCK
by John Ibbitson

Randy hates football as much as football hates him. So how could he have let Kurt Sloan con him into trying out for the football team? Now he has only two months to learn the game — and to develop shoulders.
ISBN 02-947390-X

Series Canada titles

by Paul Kropp

Amy's Wish
Burn Out
Dirt Bike
Fair Play
Hot Cars
No Way
Snow Ghost
Wild One
Baby, Baby
Dead On
Dope Deal
Gang War
Micro Man
Runaway
Take Off

by Martyn Godfrey

Fire! Fire!
Spin Out
Ice Hawk
The Beast

by John Ibbitson

The Wimp

For more information, write:

Collier Macmillan Canada, Inc.
50 Gervais Drive
Toronto, Ontario M3C 3K4
or call:
(416) 449-6030